THE ADVENTURES OF HERSHEL OF OSTROPOL

retold by
ERIC A. KIMMEL

with drawings by
TRINA SCHART HYMAN

Holiday House/New York

In memory of the Jewish community of Kolomea,
1600–1942

"Who Was Hershel?," "What Hershel's Father Did," and "The Bandit" originally appeared in another form in *Hershel of Ostropol,* Jewish Publication Society of America.

Text copyright © 1981, 1995 by Eric A. Kimmel
Drawings copyright © 1995 by Trina Schart Hyman
All rights reserved
Printed in the United States of America
First Edition
Library of Congress Cataloging-in-Publication Data
Kimmel, Eric A.
The adventures of Hershel of Ostropol / retold by Eric A. Kimmel :
with drawings by Trina Schart Hyman. — 1st ed.
p.   cm.
Summary: Stories about a clever man who lived by his wits as his
pockets were always empty.
ISBN 0-8234-1210-5
1. Ostropoler, Hershele, 18th cent. — Legends.   2. Legends, Jewish.
[1. Ostropoler, Hershele, 18th cent. — Legends.   2. Jews — Folklore.
3. Folklore.]   I. Hyman, Trina Schart, ill.   II. Title.
PZ8.1.K567Ad   1995   95-8907   CIP   AC
398.2'089924 — dc20

Contents

Who Was Hershel?

No collection of Jewish folklore is complete without at least one story about Hershel of Ostropol, or *Hershele Ostropolier,* as he is called in Yiddish, the language of Eastern European Jews.

Hershel was a real person. He lived in what is now Ukraine during the first part of the nineteenth century. As far as can be determined, he was born in the town of Balta and resided for a time in Ostropol, a tiny village, where he served as the Jewish community's *shochet* or ritual slaughterer. This indicates that Hershel must have had some education. The Jewish religion has strict rules governing the killing of animals for meat. An improperly slaughtered animal becomes *trayf*—carrion. It cannot be used for food. The shochet had to know all these rules. He also had to be able to examine the animal's internal organs, since certain diseases or irregularities would also render it trayf. Clearly, no ignoramus could ever hold such an important job. For that reason, the usual portrayal of Hershel as a man of little education may be inaccurate. Hershel is commonly pictured as being hunchbacked, as well as exceptionally ugly. Many stories about Hershel are based on this supposed fact. Since no pictures of Hershel exist, there is no way to determine if it is true.

We do know that Hershel was an exceptionally witty man. He was quick with a retort and liked to make pompous, arrogant people look foolish. Needless to say, this did not win him many friends among the rich and powerful. Hershel lost his job in Ostropol and became a *schnorrer,* a wandering beggar living by his wits as he traveled from town to town. It was during these wanderings that Hershel endeared himself to the common folk, who made him immortal by passing the stories of his jests and sayings down through the generations.

I first heard stories about Hershel when I was growing up in Brooklyn, New York. Since then I have collected them from oral sources and anthologies of Jewish folklore. My friends Hanoch Livneh and Jack Falk were kind enough to share two collections of Hershel stories with me, one in Hebrew published in Israel and a 1947 Polish reprinting of a rare Yiddish volume published in the

Soviet Union in 1921. My mother, Anne Kimmel, assisted me with the translations.

These stories reflect the values and cultural traditions of the Jewish communities of Eastern Europe. However, one does not have to be Jewish to enjoy them. Hershel, like Coyote, Anansi, B'rer Rabbit, and Tyll Eulenspiegel, belongs to all of us.

—Eric A. Kimmel
October 14, 1994

I

What Hershel's Father Did

One cold winter night Hershel of Ostropol found himself on the road far from home. He looked across the frozen fields and wondered to himself, "Where will I sleep? There isn't a village in sight." He continued walking. His stomach rumbled, for he hadn't eaten all day. His belly was as empty as his pockets.

Up ahead he saw the lights of an inn. "I'm in luck!" Hershel said. "Surely the good people in that inn will take pity on a poor wanderer." He hurried to the inn door and knocked.

The door opened. "What do you want?" the inn-keeper said in a none-too-friendly voice.

"Kind Sir, have pity on a poor stranger," Hershel began. "I have been walking all day without so much as a crust of bread to eat. I'm cold, tired, hungry, and miles from my home. Would you have a warm corner where I could spend the night? Anyplace out of the wind will do. And could you spare a bit of something for me to eat? Heaven will reward you for your good deed."

The innkeeper was a tightfisted skinflint with a per-manent frown nailed to his face. He looked Hershel over from head to foot and did not like what he saw. "I don't make the decisions around here," he told Hershel. "I'll have to ask my wife." He slammed the door in Hershel's face and went to speak to his wife in the kitchen.

"There's a man at the door. He wants a place to sleep and something to eat. What shall I tell him?"

"Does he have any money?" the innkeeper's wife asked.

"I doubt it."

"In that case," said the wife, "tell him he can sleep in the stable. But as for food, don't give him anything. I've seen his kind before. They always want a little bit of something. But once they get going, they eat like starving wolves. When the time comes to pay for what they've eaten, oh, well, that's a different story. 'I don't have any money,' is what they always say. He can sleep in the stable if he wants. But as for food, give him nothing!"

"What if he insists?"

"Tell him he got here too late. All the food is gone."

The innkeeper went back to the door and repeated these words to Hershel. "You can sleep in the stable if you want, but as for food, you got here too late. It's all gone."

"I've never heard of an inn without food," said Hershel. "Surely you have something. A bone? A fish-head? A crust of bread?"

The innkeeper folded his arms across his chest. "Didn't you hear me? I said we have nothing."

Hershel glowered. He pressed his face up close to the innkeeper's and said, "Maybe you didn't hear me. I'm hungry and I want something to eat. If I don't get something to eat, I'll do what my father did!" Hershel grabbed the innkeeper by his shirt collar and began shaking him back and forth, screaming at the top of his voice. "IF I DON'T GET SOMETHING TO EAT, I'LL DO WHAT MY FATHER DID! DO YOU HEAR ME? I'LL DO WHAT MY FATHER DID!" He shook the innkeeper, like a dog shaking a rat, shouting all the while, "I'LL DO WHAT MY FATHER DID! I'LL DO WHAT MY FATHER DID!"

The terrified innkeeper broke away and ran to the kitchen.

"What is going on out there? It sounds like a maniac is loose," his wife said.

"A m. . . m. . . maniac is loose!" the innkeeper stammered. "That fellow at the door . . . he's crazy! He said if we didn't feed him, he'd . . . he'd . . ."

"He'd what?"

"He'd do what his father did!"

"What did his father do?"

"I don't know! And I don't want to find out!" said the innkeeper. "Quick! Gather all the food we have in the house. Put it on the table. We must feed this man. Our lives depend on it!"

The innkeeper and his wife bustled around the kitchen. They gathered up all the food in the inn and piled it on the table. The innkeeper invited Hershel to help himself.

He didn't have to ask twice. Hershel sat down at the table and began to eat. He ate his way through roasts and sausages, baskets of fruit, a duck, a chicken, a whole goose, loaves of bread, pastries and sweets by the score. He ate until he couldn't hold another bite. He ate until his buttons burst. No one could eat like Hershel of Ostropol!

When Hershel finished, the innkeeper came up to him and asked very politely, "Would you like something else? Some pudding? A glass of tea?"

"Oh no," Hershel said. "I'm stuffed. I couldn't eat another morsel."

"Are you sure?"

"I am."

"In that case," the innkeeper said, "I wonder if I might ask you a question."

"Certainly!" said Hershel.

"I don't mean to be rude," the innkeeper said, "but my wife and I were wondering. What was it that your father did?"

Hershel laughed. "Since you have given me such a wonderful dinner, I will gladly answer your question. On cold dark nights when my father didn't get anything to eat . . . he went to bed hungry!"

2

The Goose's Foot

Hershel loved to eat roast goose. It was his favorite food. His favorite part of the goose were the feet.

Once, when Hershel was a small boy, his mother served roast goose for dinner. Whenever his mother cooked a goose, Hershel's parents ate one foot and his twelve brothers and sisters ate the other. Hershel was the youngest, so there were hardly even bones left by the time the foot got to him. Hershel vowed that one day he would get to eat a whole goose foot all by himself.

The next time his mother served roast goose, Hershel snatched one of the feet off the platter when no one was looking. He tucked it beneath his shirt and crawled under the table, where he ate it all by himself. Then Hershel climbed back into his chair and sat as if nothing had happened.

His father began serving dinner. He put the first goose foot on his plate. He looked for the other. It wasn't there.

"What happened to the other goose foot?" he asked.

Nobody knew. Hershel's father noticed a grease stain on Hershel's shirt.

"Hershel, do you know anything about the other goose foot?" his father asked suspiciously.

"No, Father," Hershel replied.

"Someone must have taken it, because it isn't here."

"Maybe the goose only had one foot," Hershel said.

"Who ever saw a goose with only one foot?"

"I have. Lots of times," Hershel answered.

"Where did you see such a goose?"

"Down by the lake. I'll take you there after dinner."

As soon as the family finished dinner, Hershel led his father down to the lake.

"Now, Hershel, show me one of these one-legged geese," his father said.

Hershel looked toward the geese standing on the lakeshore. "I see one! Look over there, Father." Hershel pointed to a goose standing with one leg tucked under its body. Geese often do that, and when they do, it looks as if they have only one leg.

"Do you really think that goose only has one foot?" Hershel's father asked.

"Yes," Hershel insisted. "Can't you see?"

"I can see, but I know he doesn't have one foot. Watch, and I'll show you something." Hershel's father clapped his hands together. The startled goose raised its head. At the same time it lowered its other foot.

"Aha!" said Hershel's father. "Did you see that? The goose has two feet, just as I said. Have you anything to say for yourself now?"

Hershel blinked his eyes innocently. "Father, that's a wonderful trick! You clapped your hands and the goose grew another foot. Why didn't you do that with the goose on the table?"

3

The Bandit

Hershel once traveled as far as the city of Yampol to find work. He stayed there for an entire month, earning good wages. At the end of the month he started back to Ostropol. Along the way a peasant told him about a shortcut through the forest. Hershel decided to take it, even though he knew that bandits often lurked there.

Hershel followed the narrow path through the forest. Suddenly a frightening figure jumped out from behind a tree.

"Hand over your money!"

Hershel stared into the barrel of a pistol brandished by a fierce-looking bandit. The bandit's beard hung down to his waist. He had a sharp knife stuck in his belt and one eye.

Hershel thought his last moment had come. He begged for his life. "Mercy, Reb Bandit! Don't kill me. I have a wife and seven children waiting for me in Ostropol."

"Shut up and give me your money. If I have to say it again, you're a dead man."

Hershel emptied his pockets. The bandit took every kopeck he had. He said to Hershel, "Turn around. Don't look back until you count to two hundred."

"Wait a minute," said Hershel. "You can't leave me like this!"

"What do you mean?" the bandit asked.

"You can't go away and leave me with nothing. What will I tell my wife when I come home without my wages? She won't believe I was robbed. She'll think I lost the money, or wasted it. Have pity on me. I would rather face a hundred bandits like you than my wife, Yente, when she gets angry."

"What do you want me to do?" the bandit asked. "Shall I bash you over the head with my pistol? Shall I stab you with my knife?"

"Oh, nothing so drastic as that," said Hershel. "If you would kindly shoot a bullet through my coat, Yente would see the bullet hole and then she would believe me."

"Hold out your coat," the bandit said. Hershel held out the skirt of his long overcoat. The bandit cocked his pistol and shot a bullet through it.

"Thank you very much," said Hershel. "But I was

thinking. This coat of mine has so many holes. Yente might think this is just another moth hole. I think you should shoot another hole, just to convince her.''

"All right," said the bandit. Hershel held out his coat again. The bandit fired another bullet through it.

"That's very kind," said Hershel. "Now, if I might ask just one more favor."

"What do you want now?" the bandit growled.

"I'm sorry to be a pest. However, could you shoot just one more hole. Through my cap this time. Then Yente would be sure to believe me."

"Give me your cap," the bandit said. Hershel handed his cap to the bandit. The bandit held the cap over the muzzle of his pistol and shot a third bullet right through the crown.

"Don't ask me to shoot any more holes for you," the bandit said as he handed Hershel his cap. "I don't have any more bullets."

"No bullets?" said Hershel.

"That was my last one."

"I see. Well, if you don't have any more bullets, then I have something for you." Hershel hit the bandit on the jaw, knocking him out with one punch. He took back his money and started for home once more.

4

Money from a Table

"We have to get some money. There's nothing to eat in the house," Hershel said to his wife, Yente, one evening.

"What can we do? Whom can we turn to?" Yente asked.

"I've thought of everybody we know, and no one is better off than we are—except one person."

"Who is that?"

"Uncle Zalman."

Yente began to laugh. "Uncle Zalman? That miser? He won't give us anything. He won't even remember who you are. As the saying goes, 'Poor relatives are distant relatives.' "

"If he forgets who I am, I'll make sure to remind him." Hershel put on his coat and went to see Uncle Zalman.

Yente was wrong. Uncle Zalman remembered who Hershel was. In fact, he remembered too well.

"Go away, Hershel. I know what you want. The answer is no. I won't give you any money."

"You're making a mistake, Uncle Zalman. The quickest way to get rid of someone is to lend him money. Give me fifty rubles and I promise you'll never see me again."

"Not a chance!"

"That's all right. I was only teasing." A serious look crossed Hershel's face. He sat down next to his uncle. "I didn't come here to borrow money. I came to offer you a business opportunity."

Uncle Zalman's eyebrows lifted slightly. "What sort of opportunity?" he asked.

Hershel explained. "I'm asking you to lend me one ruble. With one ruble I can get two fine laying hens. A good hen can lay thirty eggs, so from the two hens I can expect to get sixty eggs. But I won't sell them. I'll let the hens sit on the eggs until they hatch. Now figure this, Uncle Zalman. From two hens I get sixty chickens. If I can sell each of those chickens for one ruble apiece, that adds up to sixty rubles. If we divide the money, you'll get thirty rubles. Take out the ruble you lent me and it comes to a profit of twenty-nine rubles. Even if some of those chickens turn out to be roosters, you still come out ahead. After all, you're only investing one ruble. What could be better than that?"

Uncle Zalman took a pencil from his pocket and began writing figures on a scrap of paper. "Hershel, you're right. This is a brilliant idea. We'll both be rich," he said at last. Uncle Zalman opened his money box and took out a ruble. "Here you are. I'll come by in a few weeks to see how our investment is doing."

"You won't be sorry. I guarantee it." Hershel put the money in his pocket and walked to the chicken market where he bought two fine fat hens. He took them to the shochet, had them plucked and cleaned, and brought them home to Yente to cook. That night Hershel and his family sat down to a fine dinner of roast chicken.

A week later Uncle Zalman came by. "How are the chickens? Are they laying eggs yet?" he asked Hershel.

"Oy, Uncle Zalman! It hurts me to tell you this. The hens are no more."

"What do you mean? What happened to them?"

"A terrible tragedy. The hens were in the yard, scratching in the dirt as hens do, when a big dog came along and barked at them. You know how foolish hens are. Instead of flying up on the roof where they would be safe, the foolish birds were so frightened they fell over. I ran out and chased the dog away, but by then it was too late. The hens were dead. They died of fright. I buried them in the backyard. I even said a prayer for their foolish little souls."

"Are you crazy? Who cares about a couple of hens? What about my ruble?" Uncle Zalman snapped.

"Don't worry," Hershel reassured him. "I thought of

a way to get your ruble back. Lend me three rubles to buy a goose. Hens are stupid birds. They're afraid of everything. But geese are brave. We won't have to worry about dogs with a goose, and geese bring more money than chickens.''

"All right," said Uncle Zalman, digging into his pockets for three rubles. "But remember, if anything happens to the goose, you're responsible."

"I give you my word. Nothing can go wrong this time."

As soon as Uncle Zalman left, Hershel hurried to the goose market and bought a fine, fat goose. He took the goose to the shochet. After it was plucked and cleaned, he brought it home to Yente to cook for dinner. That night Hershel and his family had roast goose, and he and Yente slept that night on a pillow stuffed with goose down.

Uncle Zalman came by the next week. He stared around the yard, looking for the goose. "Where is it?" he asked Hershel.

"Oy, Uncle Zalman!" Hershel cried, shaking his head. "I have bad news to tell you. Come inside and we'll talk."

Uncle Zalman followed Hershel inside the house. They sat down at the table.

"Well? What happened to the goose? What did you do with my money?"

Hershel let out a deep sigh. "Uncle Zalman, I don't know what to say. It was another unforeseen tragedy. The hens were too timid, but the goose was afraid of nothing. That was the poor bird's downfall. A wagon came by. The foolish goose flew over the fence and attacked it. The wagon rolled over her and broke her neck. That was the end of our goose, and the end of your three rubles. But don't worry, Uncle Zalman. I have another plan that is sure to work."

"It will have to work without me," Uncle Zalman said. "I'm not throwing good money after bad. Give me the four rubles I lent you and we're done. You can find someone else to finance your crazy schemes."

"I'm sorry, Uncle Zalman. You'll have to wait. I don't have any money to pay you," said Hershel.

"What do you mean you can't pay me! I'm not leaving until I get my four rubles." Uncle Zalman started pounding on the table. "Do you hear me! Give me my four rubles! I want my money!"

"Uncle Zalman, please. Don't pound so hard. The table is old. You'll break it."

"I don't care if I break it!"

"Oh, yes you do!" Hershel replied. "I just thought of another plan to get back your money. This one is sure to work, but to carry it out I need this table—and a little help from you."

"What kind of help?"

"A small loan."

"Never!" Uncle Zalman said.

"Then you may never see your money again. Don't be so stingy, Uncle. You know very well that if you want to catch fish, you have to bait the hook."

Uncle Zalman considered that for a moment. Finally he said, "All right, Hershel. But if this scheme doesn't work, you will never see another kopeck from me. How much money do you need?"

"How much do you have in your pockets?"

Uncle Zalman emptied his pockets on the table. "Three rubles and seventy-eight kopecks."

"That's perfect!" Hershel opened a drawer and took out a hammer, a nail, a piece of string, and a little cloth sack. As Uncle Zalman watched, he turned the table over and hammered a ruble into each of the three cracks on the underside of the table. He put the seventy-eight kopecks into the little sack, tied it up with a piece of string, and nailed it to the table bottom. As soon as that was done, Hershel picked up the table and carried it out the door.

"Where are you going?" Uncle Zalman called after him.

"I'm going to get us some money."

"How can you get money from a table?"

Hershel laughed. "You'll see."

Hershel carried the table all the way through town, down the road, and far out into the countryside. Suddenly he heard the sound of a carriage coming up behind him. Hershel stepped aside to let the carriage go by. It came up alongside him and stopped.

A man leaned out the carriage window. "Hershel, where are you going with that table?" It was Count Potocki, the richest man in the county and, next to Uncle Zalman, the stingiest.

Hershel touched his cap politely. "Good day to you, Count Potocki. Where am I going with this table? I'm taking it to the market in Miropol."

"That's five miles away. Why go through all the trouble? Can't you sell it in Ostropol?"

"Nobody in Ostropol can afford to buy it."

"That broken-down table? How much are you asking for it?"

"Three hundred rubles."

Count Potocki gasped. Then he began to laugh. "Three hundred rubles for a cracked table with a broken leg? You're crazy!"

"Not as crazy as you think," Hershel said. "I'll admit this table doesn't look like much. What makes it valuable is not what it looks like but what it does."

"What does it do?" Count Potocki asked.

Hershel tiptoed over to the carriage window and whispered in Count Potocki's ear. "This table gives money."

"A table that gives money? Now I know you've lost your wits," Count Potocki said.

"It's true, whether you believe it or not," Hershel said. "Watch closely. You may change your mind." Hershel set the table on the ground. He made a fist and struck the table hard over one of the cracks, at the same time saying, "Table, give money!"

A ruble dropped from the crack. Count Potocki couldn't believe his eyes. He jumped out of the carriage, picked up the ruble, and examined it. "It's real!" he cried, amazed. Turning to Hershel, he said, "Do that again!"

Hershel made a fist and hit the table a second time. "Table, give money!" A second ruble dropped to the ground.

"It does give money! Unbelievable! Would it work for me?" the count asked.

"Go ahead and try," said Hershel.

Count Potocki banged his fist on the table. "Table, give money!" he shouted so loud he frightened his horses.

The third ruble dropped in the dirt. "Astonishing!" Count Potocki exclaimed. "I must have this table. You were going to sell it for three hundred rubles? I'll give you five."

"Five hundred rubles!" Hershel's eyes opened wide as Count Potocki handed him the money. "Thank you, Count. You're very generous. Shall I put it in the carriage for you?"

"Don't bother," Count Potocki said. "This table isn't going anywhere. I'm not going to stand around banging out rubles one at a time. I'll get my money now." He called to his coachman. "Grisha, bring me the ax from the toolbox!"

"Count Potocki, what are you doing!" Hershel cried as the count took the ax from his coachman and raised it over his head.

"Step aside, Hershel! It's my table. I bought it. I can do what I like."

Count Potocki swung the ax. Again and again it smashed into the table, chopping it to bits. The count flung the ax aside. He fell to his knees and scrabbled among the splinters, searching for rubles. All he found was a cloth sack tied with a string. He opened it. Inside were seventy-eight kopecks.

"What is this?" Count Potocki asked Hershel.

Hershel shook his head in sorrow. "Oh, Count! Do you realize what you've done? A chicken lays eggs, but when a butcher kills a chicken and cuts it open, he doesn't find eggs inside. He finds a little sack with tiny seeds that would have become eggs if the chicken had lived. It's the same with this table. If you had spared its life, it would have given you ruble after ruble for years to come. Now all you have is a tiny sack of kopecks which would have grown into rubles had you been more patient."

Count Potocki cursed and swore and tore his hair, but what could he say? Hershel had tried to warn him. The count had no one to blame but himself. As soon as he drove off, Hershel walked back to Ostropol with five hundred rubles jingling in his pockets.

When he got back home he counted out a hundred rubles for Uncle Zalman. "Hershel, maybe you should keep this money. Go out and buy more tables. We'll be millionaires!" the old man exclaimed with delight.

Hershel shook his head. "Don't be silly, Uncle Zalman. Who ever heard of making money from a table?"

5

Potatoes!

Rabbi Israel, Ostropol's chief and only rabbi, was a kindly man who cared deeply about the town's poor. Every day he made his rounds, collecting food and money from those who had something to give and using it to provide one free meal a day at the synagogue for all who were hungry.

However, the number of those with something to give was small and the number of those in need was endless. Rabbi Israel had to stretch his meager funds to provide for all. On most days he could provide only the cheapest food: potatoes.

The poor people of Ostropol ate potatoes every day at the synagogue, except on holidays, when they got potato pudding. They made up a song about it:

Monday—potatoes! Tuesday—potatoes!
Wednesday and Thursday—potatoes!
Friday, for a special treat, potatoes do we get to eat.
Saturday and Sunday—potatoes!

Hershel and his family often found themselves guests at Rabbi Israel's table. One day, after weeks of potatoes, Hershel called to Rabbi Israel, "Rabbi, what blessing do we say over these potatoes?"

Rabbi Israel answered, "Why, Hershel, you know the answer to that. We say, 'Blessed be the fruit of the earth,' just as we always do."

"I know that, Rabbi," Hershel replied. " 'Blessed be the fruit of the earth' is the blessing we make when the potatoes come out of the ground. I want to know what blessing we should say when the potatoes are coming out of our ears!"

Rabbi Israel got the point. He promised to find something better than potatoes.

The next day, when Hershel and all the poor people in Ostropol arrived at the synagogue, Rabbi Israel announced that they were going to have a special treat. Mendel the fishmonger had donated two dozen fine fish. There was going to be fish for everyone.

But when the fish was placed on Hershel's plate, he noticed something peculiar. "Something smells bad, and I know it's not me," he whispered to his neighbors. He tasted a piece of the fish. "Ugh! No wonder Reb Mendel gave this fish away. It's ancient. If it were any older, it would have a beard."

The other poor people agreed. "This fish is so old it must go back to King Sobieski's time," one said.

"If not before," the others agreed. "What can we do? Rabbi Israel wouldn't serve us rotten fish on purpose. He must not realize how bad it is. How can we let him know without embarrassing him?"

"Leave it to me," said Hershel. Putting down his knife and fork, he lowered his ear to the plate. He pretended to listen carefully. Then he turned his head and whispered a few words to the fish.

Rabbi Israel watched from the head of the table. "What are you doing, Hershel?" he asked.

"I'm talking to the fish," Hershel told him. "I asked where he was from."

"And what did the fish say?"

"He said he was from the Pruth River. He asked where he was now. I told him, 'Ostropol.' He said he never heard of it."

"And how are things in the Pruth?" Rabbi Israel went on, anticipating a good joke.

"I'll ask him." Hershel lowered his head to the table and whispered to the fish again. Looking up at Rabbi Israel, he said, "The fish says how should he know? It's been months since he was there."

Rabbi Israel's face turned red. He tasted a piece of the fish, made a face, and ordered that it be removed at once. He apologized to all the poor people, promising them another dinner as soon as it could be prepared.

Rabbi Israel kept his promise. A second dinner was soon on the table. What was it?

POTATOES!

6

The Miracle

Times were bad. Hershel's family was starving. One small onion was the only thing to eat in the house. The children lay in their beds, whimpering with hunger. Hershel's wife, Yente, sat in the corner, sighing. "Dear God, I wish I could die," she moaned. "Then there would be one less mouth to feed."

"Don't talk nonsense," Hershel said. "What does it matter how many mouths there are to feed in our house? There's nothing to eat anyway."

"We can't go on like this, Hershel," Yente said. "We

need help. Go to Rabbi Israel. He will give us something. Rabbi Israel is a good man. He never turns anyone away."

"Rabbi Israel has nothing to give," Hershel replied. "Everybody in town is suffering. There isn't enough money in the charity fund to even buy potatoes."

"If you won't go to Rabbi Israel, go to the synagogue," said Yente. "The burial society meets this afternoon. You may as well make arrangements to bury us because if we don't get some food or money soon, we are not going to be alive much longer."

The burial society! An excellent idea. The burial society always had money for poor people. The problem was they had to be dead to get it. "Yente," Hershel said, "get into bed, close your eyes, and stay there until I get back. No matter what happens, don't move until I tell you." He cut the onion in half and rubbed both pieces over his eyes until they tuned fiery red and tears ran down his cheeks like waterfalls.

Rabbi Israel had just called the burial society meeting to order when Hershel burst into the room.

"Help me, brothers!" he cried between bitter sobs. "Yente is dead. She died of hunger, poor woman. There is nothing to eat in our house. I have no money to bury her. Woe is me! What will I do?"

Rabbi Israel stood up, so shocked and surprised at this terrible news that he could hardly speak. "Hershel," he said, "why did you not come to me for help?"

"Rabbi, I wanted to. Believe me. You know how proud Yente was. She would not let me. She refused to accept charity. And so . . . she died!" Hershel burst into tears. Rabbi Israel and the members of the burial society wept with him.

Rabbi Israel unlocked the burial society's cashbox. He counted out one hundred rubles. "Take this money," he told Hershel. "Buy food for your family and decent clothes to wear to Yente's funeral. We will come by later with the coffin to prepare Yente for burial."

Hershel kissed Rabbi Israel's hand. "I cannot thank you enough, Rabbi. God will bless you for this. I only wish I had come to you sooner."

"Go in peace," Rabbi Israel said.

Hershel hurried to the market. He found a large sack and filled it with food—pies, cakes, pastries, puddings, fruit, nuts, and a whole roast goose. Hershel's children had never seen so many delicacies in their lives. They could not remember a time when they had had so much to eat.

"What about me?" Yente wailed. "How much longer do I have to lie in bed? I'm starving."

"Shh!" said Hershel. "Be quiet or you'll spoil everything."

Just then they heard a knock at the door. Hershel hurried to open it. Rabbi Israel and the members of the burial society stood outside, carrying a coffin.

"We have come to prepare Yente for burial," Rabbi Israel said.

Hershel began to weep. "Not yet. I can't bear to give her up. Let her stay with us a little while longer." All the children began crying.

"Be strong, Hershel," Rabbi Israel said. "Don't

mourn for Yente. She is in paradise with the angels. All her earthly troubles are over."

"What about me? My troubles are just beginning. Who will care for my motherless children? How will I live without my beloved Yente? There must be some way to bring her back to life."

Rabbi Israel tried to console him. "Hershel, be brave. We must accept what God has decreed. Only He can restore the dead to life. It is true that the two prophets, Elijah and Elisha, revived people who were dead. But that happened long ago in the days of the Bible. Elijah and Elisha were great and holy men. There is no one like them today."

"Can't we try, Rabbi?" Hershel asked. "If we pray hard enough, God might work a miracle."

"If God wills it, anything is possible," Rabbi Israel said. "Let us pray." Hershel, the members of the burial society, and Rabbi Israel gathered around Yente's bedside. Rabbi Israel placed his hands on Yente's forehead and began to pray. "Master of the Universe, Creator of all beings, have mercy on our sister Yente. Restore her to life, if it be Your Will. Amen."

"Amen," everyone said. Nothing happened. Yente lay motionless on the bed with her eyes shut tight.

"I will try again," said Rabbi Israel. Once more he began to pray. "Master of the Universe, Ruler of the Heavens and the Earth, have mercy on our brother Hershel, on his poor motherless children. Restore their beloved Yente to them, if so be Your Will. Amen."

Everyone said amen. But again, nothing happened.

Rabbi Israel turned to Hershel. "It is useless. God's Will cannot be changed. We must accept that it is for the best."

"Let me try, Rabbi," Hershel said. He raised his eyes to heaven. "God, I know You meant well, but You had no right to take our Yente. Give her back. We need her. As for you, Yente, I know you are enjoying paradise, but it is time to come home. Come back to life."

Yente's eyelids fluttered open. She sat up in bed. "Hershel," she exclaimed, "I'm alive. It's a miracle!"

The members of the burial society looked first at Yente, then at Rabbi Israel, then at Hershel, then back to Rabbi Israel again. "Rabbi! Can we believe our eyes? Have we witnessed a miracle?"

Rabbi Israel stared long and hard at Hershel. In the end he shrugged his shoulders. "Who am I to say? If one prays hard enough, and if God wills it, then anything is possible. I believe that miracles do happen."

Even in Ostropol.

7

An Incredible Story

Hershel stopped by the village tavern one afternoon to see his friends and hear the latest news. He found the tavern full of people.

"What's going on?" he asked the tavern keeper.

"It's Count Potocki waving his money around, making fools of everyone as he always does," the tavern keeper said.

Hershel made his way to the front of the crowd. He saw Count Potocki sitting at a table, red-faced and merry from drinking vodka. The count looked up. He pointed to Hershel. "Now here's someone who knows how to tell a real story!" He motioned to Hershel to sit down next to him.

"You know how I love a good story, and I know that you always tell a good one," the count said to Hershel. "So I'd like to make a little bet." He reached into his pocket and dropped ten hundred-ruble coins into a dish on the table. "That's a thousand rubles. If you can tell me a story so ridiculous that I can't believe it, that money is yours."

Hershel's eyes opened wide. A thousand rubles for telling one story! What could be easier? Hershel was the best storyteller in the county. That money was as good as in his pocket.

"I accept," said Hershel. "Are you ready to listen?"

"I'm all ears," said Count Potocki.

Hershel began.

"Long ago, before I was born, when your father was still a baby, I took a job working for your great-great-grandson. He had a herd of bees. Every morning I led the bees to pasture by the river. In the afternoon I led them home. I milked the honey from them, put it in a churn, and churned it into honeycake. I did this for several years." Hershel stopped. He looked at Count Potocki, waiting for him to say, "I don't believe it."

But Count Potocki nodded and said, "I think that could happen."

Hershel continued.

"One afternoon I led the bees back, but when I counted them, I realized one was missing. I hurried to the river to find the missing bee. I saw her on the other side. She had swum across. A pack of wolves was attacking her. The bee fought bravely. Every time she struck a wolf with her stinger it fell down dead. But more wolves kept coming. I knew that if I didn't help that poor bee she would surely die. There wasn't time to swim over, so I picked myself up by my beard, whirled myself around three times, and flung myself across the river. I landed on my feet, right in the middle of the wolf pack." Hershel paused.

"Go on," Count Potocki said. "That's a good story. I believe it."

Hershel began again.

"The biggest wolf charged at me with its jaws wide open to swallow me up. But I wasn't afraid. I stuck my hand inside his mouth, grabbed him by the tail, and pulled him inside out. The other wolves became frightened when they saw what happened to their leader. They put their tails between their legs and fled. I went over to see what I could do for the poor bee. Alas, she was dead! One of the wolves had jumped in her mouth and eaten his way out again. Nothing remained but her shell." Hershel stopped.

"I believe that," said Count Potocki.

Hershel frowned, but continued.

"Since there was nothing I could do for the bee, I picked myself up by the beard once more and threw myself back across the river. I started walking to your great-great-grandson's house to tell him what happened to the bee. I was almost there when I realized he wasn't as trusting as you are, Count Potocki. He might not believe me, so I decided I had better go back to collect the bee's shell to show him.

"However, the wolves had returned while I was gone

and they had eaten what was left of the bee. All I could find were the creature's bones. What bones they were! The rib bones went all the way up to the sky and disappeared among the clouds." Hershel paused, waiting for Count Potocki to say something.

"What amazing things happen in this world!" the count said.

Hershel sighed, and continued the story. "I thought I would like to see what lay above the clouds, so I started climbing up the bee's rib bone. I climbed and climbed. I think I climbed for two or three days. Whenever I got hungry, I broke off pieces of cloud and ate them. They tasted like honeycake. When I got thirsty, I dipped my hat into a cloud and drank the rainwater. When I got sleepy, I lay down among the clouds and closed my eyes. It was like sleeping on a warm featherbed.

"Finally I came to a rolling green meadow high above the clouds. I stepped onto the grass. I saw a man sitting under a tree eating raisins and almonds. I asked him what place this was. He gave me a strange look and said, 'Don't you know? You're in heaven.' "

"I would like to visit heaven someday. Maybe I could find a bee's rib bone," Count Potocki said.

Hershel continued.

" 'How lucky I am,' I said to myself. 'Not many people get the chance to see heaven while they're still alive.' I decided to have a look around. I started walking across the meadow. After a while I came upon three angels sitting on the grass playing cards. They invited me to play. We played three hands, and I won them all. The angels gave me their halos. I was surprised to see they were solid gold. I put them in my pocket and began walking away. But the angels followed me. 'Come back. You cheated us!' they began yelling.

"I knew it was time to leave. I started running. The angels came after me. They could fly much faster with their wings than I could run with my legs, but I had a good start and just managed to keep ahead of them. I reached the end of the meadow and jumped onto the bee's rib bone. I slid back the way I came, all the way down through the clouds."

Hershel stopped and waited for Count Potocki to say something.

"Go on," said Count Potocki. "I want to hear the end of this fascinating true story."

Hershel scratched his head. He wiggled his ears. He fiddled with the buttons of his coat. Then he began again.

"I slid for three days and three nights, going faster and faster. I was going so fast that my own shadow couldn't keep up with me. It was two days behind when I hit the bottom. By then I was going so fast I couldn't stop. I went right through the ground and continued going down, down, down until I came to another place. I don't have to tell you its name. It was dark and smoky. It smelled of sulfur and charcoal, with little lights flickering on and off everywhere. A terrible moaning and groaning filled the thick air. I started walking, looking for a way out. A devil with two heads came up to me and said, 'What are you doing here?' He tried to grab me with his claws, but I took out one of the angels's halos and shook it at him. The devil jumped back. He started to yell and scream, but I knew he had no power over me. As long as I had those halos in my pocket, I was safe.''

"That's very true," said Count Potocki.

Hershel went on.

"I continued walking. Those devils got out of my way when they saw me coming. I hoped that sooner or later I would find somebody who knew the way out. I didn't trust those devils to tell me the truth. After a while I came to a pigsty. It was full of giant devil pigs rolling around in mud and pig slop. A voice cried out. I looked and saw an old woman tied to a stake in the middle of the pigsty. She was covered with filth from head to foot, and the pigs were nibbling her toes."

"Tsk, tsk," said Count Potocki, "to think that such terrible things can happen."

Hershel continued.

"I took out my halos and drove the pigs away. Then I untied the poor woman and carried her out of the sty. I wiped the filth off her face with my handkerchief. To my surprise, I recognized her. It was your poor dead mother, Countess Potocki."

Count Potocki gasped.

" 'Countess Potocki,' I said, 'what are you doing here?'

" 'Alas, Hershel,' she answered, 'this is the punishment for my sin.'

" 'What sin did you commit to deserve such terrible punishment?' I asked her."

Count Potocki leaned forward. "What did she say?"

Hershel raised his voice so everyone in the tavern could hear.

"She said, 'My sin was bringing my son, that rascal Count Potocki, into the world.'"

"You liar!" Count Potocki shouted. "What a ridiculous story! I don't believe a word of it."

"Aha!" said Hershel, sweeping the coins into his pocket. "I win!"

8

The Cow

Hershel had a friend, a peasant named Ivan, who was as clever as he was. Hershel and Ivan enjoyed matching wits with each other. Sometimes Hershel got the better of Ivan. Sometimes Ivan got the better of Hershel.

One day Hershel's wife, Yente, gave him a purse containing thirty rubles. "I've been saving this money for a long time," Yente said. "I want to use it to help our family. Hershel, take this money to market and buy a cow. Be sure to get one that gives a lot of milk. That way we will never go hungry. We can drink the milk and make cheese to sell to our neighbors."

"That is a fine idea, Yente," Hershel said. "There's only one problem. A good milk cow costs a lot more than thirty rubles."

"Do the best you can. Maybe you can find a bargain," Yente said.

Hershel hurried to the market. He looked over the cows that were being offered for sale. Just as he feared, a good milk cow cost at least a hundred rubles. He and Yente would have to save a lot more money before they could drink milk and eat cheese.

As Hershel turned around to go home, he saw his friend Ivan coming toward him, leading a scrawny, under-sized cow by a rope around her neck. "I wonder if Ivan's cow is for sale," Hershel thought. "She doesn't look like much, but if she gives milk, it doesn't matter. Besides, Ivan is my friend. Maybe he will let me have the cow for a good price."

Hershel walked up to Ivan. "Hello, Ivan."

"Hello, Hershel."

"Is your cow for sale?"

"Why else would I bring her to market?"

"I want to buy a good milk cow, but I don't have a lot of money."

"How much do you have?"

"Thirty rubles."

"I'll sell you this cow for thirty rubles," said Ivan.

"It's a deal!" said Hershel. "But before I buy this cow I have to ask you some questions. Does this cow give milk?"

"Hmmm," said Ivan.

"What does that mean?"

"She gives less than some. More than others."

Hershel scratched his head. "I don't know. It took Yente a long time to save these thirty rubles. Maybe I better look around some more."

Ivan took Hershel by the arm. "Hershel, aren't we friends? You can trust me. If anything I've told you about this cow turns out not to be true, you can bring the cow back and I'll return your money. What could be fairer than that?"

"You're right," Hershel agreed. He paid Ivan the thirty rubles and led the cow home. Yente put the cow in the shed behind the house. They gave the cow water to drink and hay to eat.

"She looks like a good cow," Yente said. "She'll give lots of milk once we fatten her up."

"If not, I can always bring her back to Ivan," Hershel said.

Hershel and Yente got up at dawn to milk the cow. Hershel pulled at the cow's udder. A thin stream of milk squirted into the milk pail. Then it stopped. Hershel pulled harder, but no milk came.

"Let me try," said Yente. "I grew up on a farm. I know how to milk cows." Yente sat down on the milking stool. She tugged at the cow's udder every way she knew, but only a few more drops of milk dribbled out.

Hershel and Yente looked at the milk on the bottom of the pail. There was less than a teaspoon.

"Some milk cow!" Hershel grumbled.

"Maybe she's nervous. We'll give her time to get used to her new home," Yente said. "But if she doesn't start giving milk soon, you'll have to take her back to Ivan."

"Don't worry, Yente. Ivan promised he would return my money," Hershel said.

For the next two weeks Hershel and Yente did everything they could to make the cow feel at home. They kept her stall warm and dry. They filled her drinking pail with fresh water twice a day. They fed her the best hay. Nothing helped. The cow gave no more milk than before.

"That's enough. What good is a cow that gives no milk? I'm taking this cow back to Ivan," Hershel said.

Yente looked worried. "Are you sure Ivan will give you back your money?"

"Of course! Ivan and I are old friends. Besides, he assured me the cow was a good milker. He told me that if anything he said about this cow turned out not to be true, I could have my money back."

Hershel tied a rope around the cow's neck and led her toward the market. Along the way he saw Ivan coming toward him.

"Hello, Hershel! How do you like your new cow?" Ivan called out.

"I don't like her at all. I want my money back. Nothing you told me about this cow is true."

"Why, Hershel, what makes you say that?"

"Remember? Two weeks ago at the market, I asked if this cow gave milk. You said she was a good milker."

Ivan took a step back. "Now wait a minute, Hershel! Don't put words in my mouth. I never said she was a good milker. You asked me if the cow gave milk. I said, 'Of course!' She's a cow, isn't she? Cows give milk. What did you expect? Wine?"

"No, Ivan, I didn't expect wine. But I did expect to get

more than a teaspoon of milk in two weeks, especially after you told me this cow gave more milk than some and less than others."

"And doesn't she give more than some and less than others?"

"I can't think of any cow that gives less than a teaspoon of milk in two weeks!" Hershel shouted.

"I can. A calf." Ivan began to laugh.

Hershel had to admit that Ivan had gotten the best of him. "All right, Ivan, you win. Now take back your cow and give back my money, as you promised."

"I will do no such thing," Ivan said. "When you bought the cow I told you that if anything I said about her turned out not to be true, you could have your money back. Show me one thing I said that isn't true. The cow gives milk, doesn't she? Maybe not as much as you'd like, but you got at least a few drops out of her. She gives more than some but less than others, just as I said. I didn't tell a lie, so I don't have to give back your money. Next time, my friend, you will do well to remember that wise saying, 'Don't go to market with your eyes closed.'"

"There's another old saying I should have remembered," Hershel grumbled to himself as he led the cow home. "'When a crook kisses you on the mouth, count your teeth.'"

Yente burst into tears when Hershel told her what had happened.

"Woe is me! It took two years to save that money. Now it's gone."

"Dry your tears, Yente," Hershel said. "Ivan thinks he's so clever. Wait and see. This story isn't over yet."

For the next two weeks Hershel cared for the cow as if she were made of gold. He brushed and combed her every day until her coat shined. He rubbed her hooves with tallow so that they gleamed like a pair of new boots. The cow gave no more milk than before, but she looked wonderful. She was the grandest cow in the village.

One morning, while Hershel was leading the cow to pasture, he happened to meet Ivan. The peasant could hardly believe his eyes. Was this the same scrawny cow he had sold Hershel a month ago?

"Hello, Hershel," Ivan said.

"Hello, Ivan," Hershel replied.

"That little cow has turned into a fine-looking animal."

"I have you to thank for that, Ivan. Remember when I tried to return her to you and you wouldn't take her? You don't know what a favor you did me. All the cow needed was proper food and good care. She's turned into a splendid beast."

"Does she give a lot of milk?"

"More than some, less than others."

"Tell me the truth, Hershel. How much milk does she really give?"

"Would you believe me if I told you more than three buckets?"

Ivan's eyes opened wide. "Three buckets of milk in one day? This cow is a champion."

Hershel smiled.

"Hershel, I hope you don't think I meant to cheat you," Ivan said. "I always meant to return your thirty rubles. I'll give them to you right now, if you still want me to take back the cow."

Hershel shook his head. "Come now, Ivan. Do you take me for a fool? Do you think I'd let you have such a cow for a mere thirty rubles?"

"How much do you want?"

"I won't take less than two hundred and fifty."

"Two hundred and fifty rubles? For a cow that gives three buckets of milk a day? That's still a bargain. I'll take it." Ivan took out his purse and counted out the money. Suddenly he stopped.

"Wait a minute. There must be a trick here. Why would you sell such a cow so cheaply?"

Hershel put his hand on Ivan's shoulder. "Trust me, Ivan, there's no trick. I'm selling you this cow at a good price because you're my friend. If you're still not sure, I want you to know that you can get your money back anytime, for whatever reason."

"I can get my money back? That settles it. I have nothing to lose." Ivan gave Hershel the money. "And I can have my money back anytime. You promise."

"Absolutely!" said Hershel as he handed the rope to Ivan. Ivan led the cow away.

One week later Ivan came knocking on Hershel's door. He had the cow with him.

"Hello, Ivan, how are you today? I'm pleased to see you're looking well," Hershel said as he opened the door.

"Don't try to charm me, Hershel. I'm returning your cow. Give me back my money."

"Is something the matter with the cow?"

"You know perfectly well what the matter is. This cow gives no more milk than she ever did. Three buckets of milk a day? What a lie!"

Hershel looked surprised. "Did I say the cow gave three buckets of milk a day?"

"That's what you said. Do you deny it?"

"My dear Ivan," Hershel said, "I must ask you not to put words in my mouth. I never said the cow gave three buckets of milk a day. If you recall, you asked me how much milk she gave and I answered, 'More than three buckets.' How much milk does a bucket give? None at all. So even if the cow only gives a drop of milk a day, that's more than you'll get out of one bucket or three buckets, or even a hundred buckets."

"Very clever, Hershel, but I still want my money back. So I'll thank you to give it to me, just as you promised."

"When did I promise that, Ivan?"

"When I bought the cow. You said I could get my money back anytime, for any reason."

"And you can. Here it is, minus the thirty rubles you swindled from me, and another thirty rubles for the lesson."

"What lesson?"

"The lesson I just taught you," Hershel said. "As the old saying goes, 'Don't spit in the well. You might have to drink from it tomorrow.'"

9

The Candlesticks

When people get old, they begin thinking about the world to come. They give to charity and spend more time doing good deeds. Not Hershel's uncle Zalman. Although he was very old and very rich, he never gave anything to charity. He might have done a few good deeds in his life, but if he did, no one remembered them.

One day Rabbi Israel came by Uncle Zalman's house asking for alms to feed Ostropol's poor. Uncle Zalman sighed.

"I would like to give you something, Rabbi, I honestly

would. But you know how poor my nephew, Hershel, is. He has a whole family to support. You understand how it is. I have my own to take care of."

"I understand," Rabbi Israel said. He certainly thought Uncle Zalman could spare a few rubles, but he was too polite to argue about it.

That evening, when the poor people of Ostropol came by the synagogue to receive a free meal, Rabbi Israel was surprised to see Hershel and his family standing at the front of the line.

"Hershel, what are you doing here?" Rabbi Israel asked.

"What do you mean, Rabbi?" Hershel replied. "My family and I are hungry. If we didn't come here, we would have nothing to eat."

"But I just spoke to your uncle Zalman. He told me he provides for you."

"Uncle Zalman?" Hershel scoffed. "He never gives us anything. We'd starve if we had to rely on Uncle Zalman."

"Excuse me, I have to speak with your uncle." Rabbi Israel hurried to Uncle Zalman's house. He pounded on the door.

"Go away," came a voice from inside. "I have nothing to give. Go to the synagogue if you want charity. Rabbi Israel will feed you."

"This is Rabbi Israel. Zalman, open this door at once. I want to speak with you."

The door opened slowly. Uncle Zalman stared out, blinking in surprise. "What do you want from me,

Rabbi?" Uncle Zalman started to say. "I told you I have nothing to give. I have to take care of my own."

Rabbi Israel stopped him before he could say another word. "If you choose not to give to charity, say so. Don't lie about it. And don't tell me you have to take care of your own. I just spoke to your nephew Hershel. He tells me you never give his family anything. Is that true?"

"Yes."

"Then please explain why the richest man in town can't afford to give a few coins to charity."

Uncle Zalman breathed a deep sigh. "Rabbi, what can I tell you? If I don't give to my own, how can you expect me to give to strangers?"

Hershel also sighed when Rabbi Israel repeated what his uncle had said. "Poor Uncle Zalman. What will become of him? He goes around in rags because he is too stingy to buy new clothes. He lives on water and dry bread because he won't spend money on food. His house is falling apart, but he won't spend money to repair it. He freezes in winter because he won't spend money on firewood. He lives worse than the meanest beggar, and yet he is the richest man in town. Of course, he never gives anything to charity. He can live on nothing, so why can't everyone else? But now he is getting old. He won't live much longer. What will happen to him after he dies?"

"He will find he can't take his money into the world to come," Rabbi Israel said. "Zalman is in for a surprise if he thinks he can buy his way into heaven."

"That's what I'm worried about," Hershel said. "Uncle Zalman has no good deeds to his credit. When the angels ask him to account for his time on earth, he will have nothing to show them. I must help Uncle Zalman. He is going to do a good deed whether he wants to or not."

Rabbi Israel shook his head. "How are you going to arrange that, Hershel?"

"I have an idea. Rabbi Israel, if you will lend me a few rubles, I promise to return them to you tenfold."

Hershel took the money Rabbi Israel lent him and went to the market, where he bought two twisted, tarnished silver teaspoons. He brought them home, bent them back into shape, and polished them until they gleamed. Then he went to visit his uncle.

"Uncle Zalman, open the door. It's your nephew, Hershel."

The door opened just a crack. "Go away. You got me in trouble with Rabbi Israel."

"You got yourself in trouble with Rabbi Israel," Hershel said. "That has nothing to do with me. I'm here because I need a favor."

"If you want money, forget it!"

"I don't need money. I only want to borrow something," Hershel said quickly before his uncle could slam the door.

"What do you want to borrow?"

"I want to borrow one of your big silver serving spoons. Yente's cousins have come to visit from Minsk. I'm ashamed for them to see how poor we are. I only need the spoon for one evening. I'll bring it back tomorrow morning."

Uncle Zalman grumbled to himself. "All right. You can borrow my spoon. But if anything happens to it, you're responsible."

"Of course," Hershel said. "Don't worry about a thing. I'll bring it to you tomorrow. I promise."

Hershel went back to his uncle's house the next morning. He laid the big silver serving spoon on the table. Beside it he placed a little silver teaspoon.

"What's this?" Uncle Zalman asked.

"This little spoon is yours. The big spoon gave birth while it was at my house. Rabbi Israel says that if one person borrows a cow from another and the cow gives birth, the calf belongs to the person who owns the cow, not the person who borrowed it. Therefore the teaspoon belongs to you."

Uncle Zalman blinked as he stared at the teaspoon. His face lit up with a big smile. He had never heard of a spoon giving birth and didn't believe such a thing could actually happen, but he had nothing against acquiring an extra silver spoon.

"Thank you very much, Hershel," Uncle Zalman said. "I am pleased to see I have such an honest nephew."

"In that case, may I ask another favor?"

"Of course! I'll do whatever I can—as long as you don't ask to borrow money."

"I don't want money," said Hershel. "I want to borrow your silver serving spoon again. Yente's aunt and her family are coming from Lemberg to visit us . . ."

"And you don't want them to see how poor you are. I

understand. And you may certainly borrow my big silver spoon again. The family honor is at stake," said Uncle Zalman. "And of course, if by chance the spoon should give birth to any little spoons, you'll bring them right to me?"

"Of course," said Hershel.

Hershel returned to his uncle's house the next morning, bringing the big silver serving spoon and a second shining teaspoon. Uncle Zalman beamed with pleasure.

"Another spoon! What good fortune! How pleased I am to have such an honest nephew."

"Thank you, Uncle," Hershel said. "And now, I hope you won't get angry if I ask you for a really big favor."

"Of course. Ask me for anything—as long as it isn't . . ."

"Don't worry, Uncle, I know you better than to ask you for money. Yente's relatives have decided to stay over for the Sabbath. Yente and I don't have proper Sabbath candlesticks. We had to sell ours long ago. I don't want to be ashamed before Yente's relatives. Could I possibly borrow your silver candlesticks?"

Uncle Zalman's silver candlesticks were a foot tall and made of solid silver. They were worth a great deal of money. Uncle Zalman frowned.

"I never let these candlesticks out of my sight. If anything should happen to them . . ."

"Don't worry, Uncle, I'll be responsible. And of course, if one of the big candlesticks should give birth to a little candlestick, I'll bring the baby right back with the mother."

"Of course," said Uncle Zalman. "I know I can trust you. You can borrow the candlesticks. Just make sure you bring them back as soon as the Sabbath is over—along with any offspring that might appear."

"Uncle, you can count on me," Hershel said as he carried the candlesticks home.

They never got that far. Hershel ran straight to market where he pawned the candlesticks for a great deal of money. Then he went to the synagogue where he gave the money to Rabbi Israel.

"This is a gift from Uncle Zalman to the poor people of Ostropol," he told the rabbi.

Rabbi Israel thanked Hershel. "I know the angels were looking down," he said. "Your uncle will be rewarded for his generous gift in heaven."

Hershel kept a few rubles for himself. With these he bought a chicken, some gefilte fish, a pair of fine white candles, and two loaves of challah bread—enough to make a fine Sabbath dinner.

Uncle Zalman sat by his front door after the Sabbath was over, waiting for Hershel to return with his candlesticks. Sunday and Monday came and went. When Hershel failed to appear, Uncle Zalman began to get worried. He pulled on his worn-out boots and his threadbare coat and went looking for his nephew. He caught sight of him in front of the synagogue, talking to Rabbi Israel.

"Hershel, where are my candlesticks?" Uncle Zalman yelled. Hershel turned to run away, but his uncle held him fast.

Hershel sighed. "Alas, Uncle! What can I say? Your candlesticks are no more."

"No more? What do you mean? Were they stolen?"

"No, Uncle. It's much worse. Your candlesticks . . . poor things . . . they died!"

"Died? What do you mean they died? How can candlesticks die?"

"It's true, Uncle. You must believe me. It happened after Sabbath was over. Yente came into the room and found them lying on the table—dead!"

"What nonsense is this! You're playing some kind of trick!" Uncle Zalman turned to Rabbi Israel. "Hershel stole my candlesticks. You can't let him get away with this. Make him give them back to me."

"You can't blame Hershel," Rabbi Israel said. "The candlesticks died. According to our law, if one person borrows a cow from another person and the cow dies of natural causes, the person who borrowed her is not responsible."

"But a candlestick isn't a living thing," Uncle Zalman protested. "A candlestick can't die. It's nonsense!"

"Nonsense, is it?" said Rabbi Israel. "And isn't it also nonsense that a spoon can give birth? You didn't complain then. You were happy to accept nonsense when you stood to profit from it. Therefore you must also accept nonsense when it is to your loss."

*　　　*　　　*

Uncle Zalman never recovered his candlesticks. However, a good deed is a good deed, even when it is done unwillingly. When Uncle Zalman died, his one good deed earned him a place in the world to come.

Which, for two mere candlesticks, is a very good bargain.

10

Hershel Goes to Heaven

Nobody lives forever. One day Hershel of Ostropol's life came to an end. His soul flew up to heaven to stand before the celestial gates. Like all human beings, Hershel had to give an account of his deeds on earth before he could be admitted to heaven.

"What is your name?" the examining angel asked.

"I am the well-beloved and holy Rabbi Israel from the town of Ostropol," Hershel told him.

"You're from Ostropol, all right," the angel said, "but you're not Rabbi Israel. We know who you are. You're Hershel."

Hershel replied, "So if you knew, why did you ask?"

"Don't be smart. Just answer the questions," the angel said. "Did you help the poor during your days on earth?"

"Certainly." Hershel went on to explain. "Ostropol is the poorest town in the district and I was the poorest person in Ostropol. You would have to look far and wide to find someone poorer than me. Every time I sat down at the table, I helped myself. If that's not helping the poor, I don't know what is."

The angel wrote down Hershel's reply. "Next question. Did you obey the Ten Commandments?"

"Absolutely!" said Hershel.

"Which commandment did you observe best?"

"The one that says, 'Thou shalt not covet thy neighbor's possessions.' My neighbors were just as poor as I was. They had nothing to covet."

"What about the Sabbath? Did you observe it faithfully?"

"No one observed the Sabbath better than me," Hershel said. "The commandment says, 'Remember the Sabbath day and keep it holy. No sort of labor shall you do.' Most people observe that commandment only one day a week. In my case, whole months went by without me doing any sort of labor."

The examining angel was about to ask the last question when a voice rang out, "Come in, Hershel. The gates of heaven are open to you. Heaven is such a solemn place. We can use the merriment you bring."

Thus did Hershel of Ostropol enter eternal life, to spread laughter and joy among the angels.

Hershel's Sayings

God must love poor people. Why else would He make so many of them?

Better a whole lie than a half-truth.

The sleigh rests in summer, the wagon in winter. The horse, never.

How to get rid of someone for good: If he's rich, ask to borrow money. If he's poor, lend him some.

What does God think of money? Look who He gives it to.

Stay out of the way of a mad dog, a runaway horse, and a fool with an education.

You can't fill a sack with holes; you can't pay your debts with tears.

With luck, who needs wisdom?

It's no disgrace to be poor, but it's no great honor either.

Never wish the doctor or the undertaker a good year.

A fool's blessing is he doesn't know he doesn't know.

Be extra careful in front of a goat, in back of a horse, and on every side of a drunkard.

It's easy to practice barbering on somebody else's beard.

If we didn't have to eat, we'd all be rich.

Better an honest slap than a false kiss.

If you are too bitter, the world will spit you out. Too sweet, and it will gobble you up.

Better to eat black bread than to dream of challah.

If God wills it, geese can sing.